BRAVE
SOLDIER JANOSH

VICTOR G. AMBRUS

OXFORD UNIVERSITY PRESS
OXFORD NEW YORK TORONTO MELBOURNE

Oxford University Press, Walton Street, Oxford OX2 6DP Oxford London Glasgow New York Toronto Melbourne Wellington Kuala Lumpur
Singapore Jakarta Hong Kong Tokyo Delhi Bombay Calcutta Madras Karachi Nairobi Dar es Salaam Cape Town

Printed in Italy

In a small village in Hungary lived the old soldier Janosh. He always wore his bright red uniform and carried his sword, and every day he swaggered down the village street.

None of the villagers had ever journeyed far from home, and they thought that Janosh, who had spent most of his life away at the wars, must be a very brave man. They liked to listen to his stories, especially the one about the time he met the great Napoleon and defeated

his army single-handed. They believed every word he said—except for the student, who occasionally let out a big sneeze. (When you sneeze at a story in Hungary, it means that you do not really believe it is true.)

But this did not stop the old soldier from telling his tale
or the rest of the villagers from paying close attention.
This is the story Janosh told.
"I was just having a quiet smoke," said Janosh, "when I
heard heavy footsteps behind me. . . ."

"I jumped on my horse—and saw a fearful sight! Making straight for me was the great Napoleon with all his fiercest Grenadiers."

"Any other man would have fled for his life, but I drew my sword and threatened them, and they began to run in all directions."

"'Send for the cannon!' roared Napoleon, riding off as
fast as his horse could carry him."

"The army came back with the biggest cannon they could find. They shot an enormous cannon ball at me—I had a job avoiding it. But it was no use. . . ."

"I was soon charging them again, and again they began to run. But I need not tell you that my horse was the fastest of all, and not one of them could escape from me.

"Yet I am a kindhearted man, and I spared their lives, even the great Napoleon's."

"In fact, we became good friends, and later we rode to Paris together. Napoleon turned into a very peaceable man and never started another war."

"He loved me so well and was so grateful to me for sparing his life that he filled my pockets with gold. And if I had not had such large holes in my pockets, I should still be the richest man among you."

The villagers listened spellbound, astonished
at Janosh's bravery—all except the student,

who again let out a most enormous sneeze.

Then the old soldier Janosh got up and went out of the door.

OSCAR the HEBRIDEAN CAT

Molly Arbuthnott

illustrated by Agnes Treherne

OSCAR THE HEBRIDEAN CAT

FIRST PAPERBACK EDITION
- 2019 -

Edit & layout Shaun Russell

Published by
Jelly Bean Books
Mackintosh House
136 Newport Road, Cardiff, CF24 1DJ
www.candyjarbooks.co.uk

Printed and bound in the UK by
4edge, 22 Eldon Way, Hockley, Essex, SS5 4AD